YUCK'S AMAZING UNDERPANTS

Yuck came downstairs to say good night. He was dressed like a superhero, wearing his underpants outside his pajamas.

"Yuck, why are you dressed like that?" Dad asked.

"These are my Amazing Underpants," Yuck said.

"They stink!" his sister, Polly Princess, told him, pinching her nose.

Yuck's underpants were dirty and crusty
and smelly. He had been wearing them every
day and every night for six weeks.

MATT AND DAVE

YUCK

YUCK'S AMAZING UNDERPANTS
AND
YUCK'S SCARY SPIDER

Illustrated by Nigel Baines

A Paula Wiseman Book
Simon & Schuster Books for Young Readers
New York London Toronto Sydney New Delhi

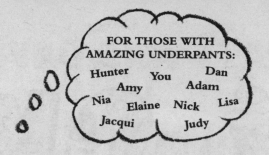

FOR THOSE WITH
AMAZING UNDERPANTS:
Hunter You Dan
Amy Adam
Nia Elaine Nick Lisa
Jacqui Judy

SIMON & SCHUSTER BOOKS FOR YOUNG READERS
An imprint of Simon & Schuster Children's Publishing Division
1230 Avenue of the Americas, New York, New York 10020
This book is a work of fiction. Any references to historical events, real people, or real locales are used fictitiously. Other names, characters, places, and incidents are products of the author's imagination, and any resemblance to actual events or locales or persons, living or dead, is entirely coincidental.
Text copyright © 2008 by Matthew Morgan and David Sinden
Illustrations copyright © 2008 by Nigel Baines
Originally published in Great Britain on October 1, 2007 by Simon & Schuster UK, Ltd.
First US edition May 2012
All rights reserved, including the right of reproduction in whole or in part in any form.
SIMON & SCHUSTER BOOKS FOR YOUNG READERS is a trademark of Simon & Schuster, Inc.
For information about special discounts for bulk purchases, please contact Simon & Schuster Special Sales at 1-866-506-1949 or business@simonandschuster.com.
The Simon & Schuster Speakers Bureau can bring authors to your live event. For more information or to book an event, contact the Simon & Schuster Speakers Bureau at 1-866-248-3049 or visit our website at www.simonspeakers.com.
Also available in a Simon & Schuster Books for Young Readers hardcover edition
The text for this book is set in Bembo.
The illustrations for this book are rendered in pencil and ink.
Manufactured in the United States of America
0812 OFF
4 6 8 10 9 7 5 3
Cataloging-in-Publication data for this book is available from the Library of Congress.
ISBN 978-1-4424-5121-6 (hc)
ISBN 978-1-4424-5122-3 (pbk)
ISBN 978-1-4424-5172-8 (eBook)
yuckweb.com

CAUTION:
YUCKY FUN INSIDE!

"They're full of germs," Mom told him.
"Go and put them in the laundry basket at
once!"

Yuck ran out of the living room. He raced straight upstairs to his bedroom and hopped into bed.

From under his pillow he pulled out a flashlight and his Superspy Magnifying Glass. He dived under the covers to investigate.

Through the magnifying glass Yuck could 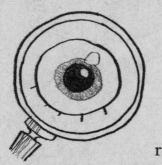 see hundreds of germs squirming and wiggling in his underpants.

They were almost ready!

Yuck reached over the side of his bed and shone his flashlight onto Swampland. He grabbed his jar of mold.

From his bedroom floor he picked up a paintbrush. It was one he'd borrowed from Polly's painting set. He dipped the paintbrush into the jar and stirred the green mold around and around.

"It's time for a midnight snack," he said, heading back under the duvet.

Yuck painted a thick blob of green mold onto his underpants, working it deep into the crusty cloth.

He painted another blob, then another. He dabbed mold all over his underpants, first on the outside and then again on the inside.

By the time he'd finished, his underpants were moldy and green.

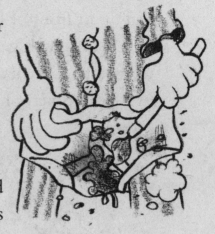

Yuck smiled. He lay down and closed his eyes, feeling the germs nibbling and wiggling, eating the mold as he drifted off to sleep.

In the morning, Yuck woke up giggling. Something was tickling him under the duvet. He threw back the covers and looked down.

Wow! His underpants were moving!

Yuck grabbed his Superspy Magnifying Glass and inspected them closely.

In the night, the germs had eaten the mold. They'd grown and multiplied. MILLIONS of them were crawling and wiggling in front of his eyes. His underpants were ALIVE with germs!

"Rockits!" Yuck said.

At that moment, his door opened.

Polly Princess came into his room.

"Get up, Yuck," she told him. "Mom says you've got to help with the cleaning!"

"CLEANING?" Yuck asked.

Mom came in behind Polly. "Your room is disgusting, Yuck," she said.

Mom started picking up the dirty underpants and socks from Yuck's floor.

"What about those ones?" Polly said, pointing to the underpants Yuck had on over his pajamas.

"No!" Yuck shouted. "You can't wash these!"

"I told you to put those in the laundry basket," Mom said. She pulled Yuck's underpants off his legs.

"But they're my—"

"Don't be silly, Yuck," Mom told him.

"They're dirty and crusty and smelly," Polly said.

"Now get dressed and come and help with the cleaning," Mom said.

She carried Yuck's underpants out with the rest of the dirty washing. Polly stuck her tongue out, then ran downstairs.

Yuck decided that when he was EMPEROR OF EVERYTHING, everyone's underpants would be dirty. It would be the LAW. Anyone who tried to clean their underpants would be bounced up and down in the WEDGIE MACHINE.

Yuck got up and put his clothes on. He

 emptied the mold from his jar into his pocket, then crept to the bathroom.

He grabbed his moldy underpants from the laundry basket, stuffed them up his T-shirt, and ran downstairs.

Mom was wiping the kitchen table.

Dad was scrubbing the kitchen floor.

Polly picked up a pink feather duster and went to dust the living room.

Yuck followed her.

He sneaked in and hid behind the sofa.

Polly dusted the ornaments.

She dusted the pictures on the walls.

Then she dusted the trophy she'd won in a coloring competition.

She stood back to admire her work. Everything looked shiny and clean. "Mom! I've finished!" she called.

While Polly went to find Mom, Yuck crept out from behind the sofa.

"Let's help her," he whispered to his underpants. Yuck dipped them into his pocket of mold, and they started wriggling in his hand.

He put them onto the mantelpiece, and they wriggled over the ornaments.

He wiped them up the wall, and they wriggled over the pictures.

He put them on Polly's trophy and they wriggled up and down the shiny silver.

They covered everything in mold.

Yuck heard Polly coming back with Mom. He grabbed his underpants and hid behind the sofa.

The door opened.

"Polly, what have you done?" Mom asked. "It's filthy in here!"

"It was clean a minute ago," Polly said.

"What a mess you've made, Polly!"

Mom snatched the pink feather duster.

"But it wasn't me!" Polly said, looking at the mess in the living room.

"Where's Yuck?" she asked.

Yuck kept very quiet.

"I thought he was helping you," Mom said.

Polly stormed out of the door.

While Mom cleaned up, Yuck sneaked out from behind the sofa. He crept to the coatrack in the hallway and watched as Polly took the vacuum cleaner out of the cupboard under the stairs. She connected the long tube and switched it on.

The vacuum cleaner began sucking up dust and dirt from the carpet.

"Let's help her," Yuck whispered to his underpants. He dipped them into his pocket of mold and they wriggled in his hand. The more mold he gave them, the more they wriggled. They were growing stronger.

Yuck placed them on the floor and they crawled out from behind the coats.

As Polly pushed the vacuum cleaner, Yuck's underpants shot straight up the tube.

The vacuum cleaner groaned.

Polly gave it a kick.

The vacuum cleaner growled.

She looked down the tube to see what was blocking it.

BANG!

Dust and dirt shot out of the end of the tube, covering Polly in a thick gray cloud.

Yuck giggled. He reached out from behind the coats and grabbed his underpants from the floor.

"Polly! What have you done now?" Mom shouted, running to see what had happened. The hallway was covered in dust. "What a mess you've made, Polly!"

Mom snatched the vacuum cleaner.

"But it wasn't me," Polly said, looking at the mess in the hallway.

"Where's Yuck?" she asked.

Yuck kept very quiet.

"I thought he was helping you," Mom said.

Polly stormed off into the kitchen.

She filled a bucket with soapy water. Then she grabbed a sponge and a rag, and went out of the front door to wash the car.

When Mom's back was turned, Yuck sneaked out from behind the coats and followed Polly outside.

Hiding behind the trash can, he watched as Polly covered the car with foam and bubbles.

She rubbed it all over. Then she rinsed the

bubbles off and started polishing the car with a rag.

Polly stood back to admire her work.

The car looked shiny and clean.

"Dad! I've finished!" she called.

While Polly went to fetch Dad, Yuck crept out from behind the trash can.

"Let's help her," he whispered to his underpants.

He dipped them into his pocket of mold, then for extra energy he dunked them in a dirty puddle.

They lapped up the stinky brown water and started wriggling.

They jumped out of Yuck's hands and onto the hood of the car. They were growing even stronger.

They crawled across the roof and up and down the doors.

They rubbed mold round and round the wheels and sloshed stinky brown water over the windshield.

Yuck heard Polly coming back with Dad. He grabbed his underpants and hid behind the trash can.

Dad looked at the car. "Polly! It's filthy!" he said.

"It was clean a minute ago," she told him.

"What a mess you've made, Polly!"

Dad snatched the rag.

"But it wasn't me!" Polly said, looking at the mess on the car.

"Where's Yuck?" she asked.

Yuck kept very quiet.

"I thought he was helping you," Dad said.

Polly stormed off through the side gate into the backyard.

Yuck followed her and hid in the bushes.

Polly fetched a broom and began sweeping the back path.

"Let's help her," Yuck said.

He filled his underpants with big balls of sticky mud. They seemed to like mud.

They wriggled and squelched, then jumped out of his hands, rustling in the bushes like an animal.

Yuck made a gap in the leaves, and his underpants hopped into position.

He stretched them like a catapult.

PING!

SPLAT!

His underpants shot sticky mud all over the kitchen window.

"Polly!" Mom shouted out. "What do you think you're doing?"

Polly turned and saw the window covered in mud.

"What a mess you've made, Polly!"

"But it wasn't me!" Polly said, looking at the mess on the window.

"Where's Yuck?" she asked.

Yuck came walking up the garden.

"Where have you been?" Mom asked.

"I've been helping Polly," Yuck said.

Polly glared at him.

"No, he hasn't," she said. "He hasn't done anything all morning."

"Come indoors now, both of you," Mom told them. "It's lunchtime."

Yuck and Polly went inside.

All through lunch Yuck hid his underpants under the table, feeding them mold from his pocket.

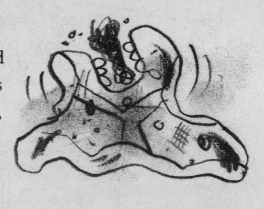

"This afternoon, I'd like you both to tidy your rooms," Mom said.

When Yuck and Polly had finished eating, Mom cleared the table.

Yuck ran upstairs and lay on his bed with his underpants.

"I think we deserve a rest," he said, opening his copy of *Oink*.

PLANET OF THE UNDERPANTS

SPACEMONKEY LOOKED OUT FROM HIS TIME MACHINE...

IT WAS 1,000 YEARS IN THE FUTURE

THERE WAS NO TRACE OF HUMAN LIFE. ONLY UNDERPANTS HAD SURVIVED.

Meanwhile, Polly was hard at work, tidying her room.

She put her clothes and toys away. She organized her books on the shelves. She ordered her pens by color, polished her mirror, and puffed up her pillows. She started making her bed.

Yuck put down his copy of *Oink*.

He sniffed. There was a tasty smell coming from downstairs. "Do you like chocolate?" he said to his underpants.

He picked them up and crept to the kitchen.

Mom had been baking. She was filling a cake tin with chocolate brownies.

Yuck crept up behind her and hid his underpants in the mixing bowl on the counter.

Mom turned around. "What are you doing, Yuck?" she said.

"You should be tidying your room."

"I've already done it," Yuck told her.

"That was very quick," Mom said.

While Mom was talking, Yuck's underpants wriggled in the mixing bowl. They were eating the leftover chocolate.

"I've been working very hard," Yuck said.

He watched as his underpants crawled from the bowl and lifted the lid of the cake tin. They jumped in and loaded themselves up with chocolate brownies.

"Can I go outside and play now, please?" Yuck asked.

"Off you go, then," Mom told him.

"Rockits!" Yuck said.

His underpants pressed the lid back on the cake tin and waddled behind the toaster.

While Mom put the cake tin in the cupboard, Yuck grabbed his underpants and ran outside.

They were full of chocolate brownies!

He carried them to the end of the yard.

"Good boy," Yuck said,

dividing the chocolate brownies into two piles, one for his underpants and the other for himself.

Yuck's underpants seemed to like chocolate very much. They gobbled the brownies in seconds, then began hopping up and down.

They raced around the garden.

"Wow!" Yuck said.

His underpants could run!

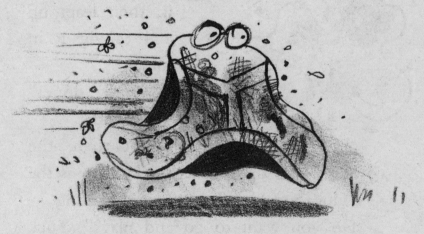

Yuck picked up a tennis ball from the lawn. "Can you fetch?" he said.

Yuck threw the ball across the yard and his underpants chased after it.

They jumped on the ball, scooped it up, and carried it back to him.

"Well done!" Yuck said, as they dropped the ball on the grass.

He gave them a pat, then picked up a Frisbee. "Can you catch?" he said.

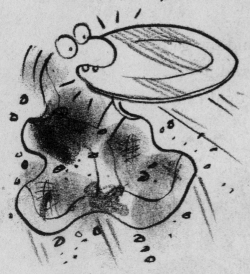

He threw the Frisbee across the yard. His underpants chased after it, then leapt up and caught it in midair.

"Well done!" Yuck said.

Just then, the corners of his underpants pricked up as the next-door neighbors' dog started barking.

"Do you want to go and play?" Yuck asked.

His underpants ran off and burrowed under the fence.

The next-door neighbors' dog was pooping.

Yuck's underpants scurried to the dog poop, jumped in it, and gobbled it up.

The underpants looked up and saw a squirrel running up a tree. They chased after it, climbing up the tree trunk and jumping from branch to branch.

A little bird saw them, flapped its wings, and took off.

Yuck's underpants started flapping too.

"Wow!" Yuck said.

His Amazing Underpants jumped off the branch and soared into the sky.

They could fly!

"Go, underpants, go!" Yuck called.

At that moment, Polly came outside. She'd finished tidying her room.

"Yuck!" she called. "Mom says you've got to come in now."

Yuck's underpants hovered above Polly's head.

"It's dinnertime," Polly called.

Yuck whistled, and his underpants dropped.

Polly screamed as they landed on her.

Mom came running out to see what had happened. "What on earth's the matter?" she asked.

"It's Yuck's stinky underpants!" Polly cried, pulling them off her head. "He threw them at me!"

Polly chucked them on the ground, and ran inside to wipe her face.

Yuck came walking up the yard.

"Put those in the laundry basket right now!" Mom told him.

"But, Mom, they're my—"

"Don't be silly, Yuck," Mom said. "Now do as you're told."

Yuck picked up his underpants and ran indoors and up the stairs.

Polly's bedroom door was open.

He peered in.

Her room was tidy.

He put his underpants on her bed.

"Wait here," Yuck said to them. "I won't be long. Have as much fun as you want."

He went back downstairs for dinner. Mom, Dad, and Polly were sitting at the table eating. Polly was looking very pleased with herself.

"Polly's tidied her room," Dad told him.

"So have I," Yuck said, sitting down.

"He's lying," Polly said. "He hasn't done anything all day!"

"I'll be inspecting your rooms after dinner," Mom told them both.

Polly smiled at Yuck.

Yuck pushed his chicken pie around his plate.

"Eat up," Dad told him.

"I'm not hungry," Yuck said.

"Come on, Yuck. If you don't eat your dinner, you can't have a chocolate brownie," Mom said.

Polly's plate was clean. She'd eaten all her chicken pie. "Can I have a brownie, please, Mom?" she asked.

Mom stood up and fetched the cake tin from the cupboard.

It was empty!

"Who's stolen the chocolate brownies?" Mom demanded.

Everyone looked at Yuck.

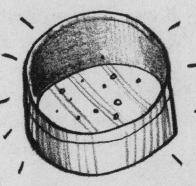

"It wasn't me," Yuck said. "I've been cleaning and tidying."

Mom went to inspect his room.

Yuck jumped up and raced after her. Polly followed him.

As Mom opened Yuck's bedroom door, she coughed. "It's disgusting in here!"

"But that's the way I like it," Yuck said.

"You haven't tidied at all," Mom told him.

Suddenly there came a scream from Polly's room.

Mom ran to see what had happened.

Polly was standing in her doorway, shaking.

Her clothes and toys were scattered over the floor. Her books had fallen off the shelves. The caps were off her pens and ink was leaking on the carpet. Her pillows were torn and there were feathers everywhere. Her mirror was smeared with green mold, and her duvet was brown with chocolate.

"Polly!" Mom said. "It's filthy in here!"

"It was clean when I left it," Polly said.

"What a mess you've made!"

"But it wasn't me," Polly said.

Just then, she saw Yuck's underpants lying on her pillow.

"What are they doing in here?" she asked.

Yuck's underpants had been playing.
Mom picked them up.

"Yuck!" she shouted.

Yuck was giggling
in his room.

Mum took his
underpants to the
bathroom.

When she came out,
Yuck crept in and
grabbed them from the
laundry basket.

"Well done!" he said.

But as he turned to leave, Mom and Polly
were standing in the doorway.

"Not so fast!" Mom said.

"I told you he's been up to something,
Mom."

"Put those underpants back, Yuck!" Mom
told him.

"But Mom, they're my—"

"Don't be silly," Mom said. She grabbed
them and stuffed them back in the basket.

And when it was bedtime, Mom locked Yuck in his bedroom to make sure that he didn't take them out again.

She turned the key. "First thing in the morning, your underpants are going in the wash," she said.

"They're going to GET IT," Polly whispered at the door.

Yuck rattled the door handle.

"If Mom washes them, they'll DIE," he said.

That night, Yuck dreamed he was the only soldier at Fort Underpants. He was surrounded by washing machines, attacking him from all sides, bombarding him with bubbles. Then, all of a sudden, he heard the call of a trumpet. From a faraway hill he saw hundreds of underpants riding toward him on horses. The cavalry was coming to save him!

In the morning, Yuck woke up and jumped right out of bed. He banged on the door for someone to let him out.

The key turned. It was Polly. "You're too late," she said, grinning.

Yuck ran to the bathroom. The laundry basket had gone.

He ran downstairs and burst into the kitchen. The washing machine was spinning. The clothes were whirring round and round.

"No!" Yuck shouted.

Dad was sitting at the table reading the newspaper. "What's the matter, Yuck?" he asked.

"My Amazing Underpants are DEAD!" Yuck said.

The washing machine stopped and Mom pulled out the clothes.

Yuck could see lots of pairs of underpants, and all of them were CLEAN.

Polly came into the kitchen and stuck her tongue out at Yuck.

"I'll hang up the laundry for you, Mom," she said.

"Good girl, Polly."

Dad put his newspaper down. "What do you mean, your underpants are dead, Yuck?" he asked.

Yuck looked at the newspaper on the table. He read the headline on the front page: UFO SPOTTED IN THE NIGHT.

Beneath it was a picture of some-

thing flying in the sky—something shaped like a pair of underpants.

Yuck ran out of the kitchen.

He raced upstairs to the bathroom. Looking closely, he could see a trail of green mold from the floor to the window.

The window was open.

Yuck ran to his room and opened his curtains. There, waiting for him outside, were his Amazing Underpants!

They saw him and started flapping.

"You escaped!" Yuck said. "You're alive!"

They were moldy and muddy and covered in chocolate.

Yuck opened his window and gave them a great big hug.

"I'll NEVER let them clean you," he said.

"You're the best underpants in the whole wide world."

Then he looked down.

In the yard, Polly was hanging the laundry on the line to dry. Her basket was full of clean underpants.

"Let's help her," Yuck said.

He waited until Polly had gone back indoors, then released his underpants into the air. They flapped and circled high above the yard.

"Now!" he called.

His underpants swooped down and landed on the clothesline. They crawled along it, stopping at each clothespin. When-ever they passed a  pair of underpants, they wriggled and shook, sprinkling a shower of germs.

"Good boy," Yuck called.

He watched as all the underpants on the line began twitching. Then he whistled and his Amazing Underpants flapped and took off.

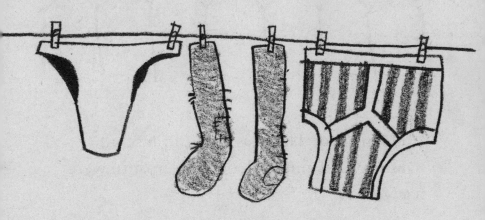

"More!" Yuck called, pointing to the next-door neighbors' clothesline.

His underpants flew across to next-door's laundry and covered it in germs. Then they flew to the clothesline in the next yard, and then the next. On every clothesline in the neighborhood, Yuck could see underpants starting to twitch.

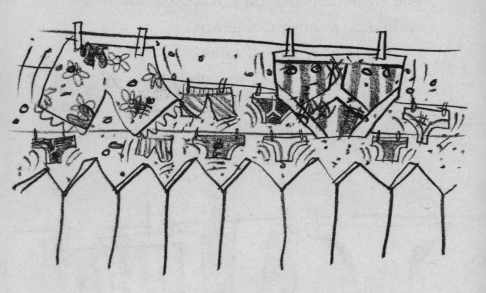

He giggled. This was going to be fun.

He waited until all the underpants were ready.

"I think the laundry's dry," he called down the stairs.

"I'll bring it in, Mom," Polly said.

She carried the empty basket outside, and started unpinning the laundry from the line.

But something was wrong.

"Mom!" she called. "All the underpants have gone!"

At that moment, the sky turned dark as a big black cloud passed across the sun.

Polly looked up.

The big black cloud began flapping.

"Mom!" she called. "Help!"

Flying above her was a huge flock of underpants!

The sky was FULL of them! Dirty, crusty, smelly underpants!

Polly turned to run.

The underpants dived.

Pair after pair landed on her, hundreds of them, covering her in germs.

"Get them off me!" Polly shrieked. "Get them off me!"

Mom ran out to see what was happening. The garden was covered with washing. There were underpants everywhere. Polly was rolling on the ground.

"Polly! What have you done?"

"It wasn't me!" Polly screamed.

Underpants were crawling all over her. Germs were wriggling in her hair and her clothes.

Dad ran out from the kitchen. "Polly, what a mess you've made!" he said.

"It wa—" Polly's mouth was full of underpants.

At that moment, Yuck whistled from his bedroom window.

The dirtiest, crustiest, smelliest pair of underpants crawled off Polly's head.

Mom and Dad watched in astonishment as they took off and flew up to Yuck, doing a loop-the-loop.

"That's incredible!" Dad said.

"That's amazing!" Mom said.

Yuck was laughing.

"I told you," he said. "They're my Amazing Underpants!"

YUCK'S SCARY SPIDER

Yuck and his sister, Polly Princess, were sitting at the kitchen table eating their breakfast. A big, fat, hairy, scary spider came crawling under the back door.

Yuck smiled.

"What are you smiling at?" Polly asked him.

The spider scurried across the kitchen floor and disappeared under Polly's chair.

"Nothing," Yuck said, giggling.

"What's so funny?" Polly said.

Yuck pretended to drop his spoon. He bent down under the table and saw the spider climbing onto Polly's shoe. It crawled over her laces and crept up her sock.

Polly scratched her ankle. She could feel something tickling her.

The spider ran inside her pants and up her leg.

"Aaaggghhh!" she screamed, jumping off her chair.

Yuck was laughing.

Polly shook her leg. "A spider! There's a spider in my pants."

Mom and Dad came dashing in.

"What's going on in here?" Mom asked.

"A spider!" Polly screamed. "A big, fat, hairy, scary spider!"

The spider dropped out of Polly's pants and scurried across the floor.

"Where did it go?" Dad asked, hunting under her chair.

Mom searched in the cupboards and behind the toaster. "It's gone," she said.

Just then, something big, fat, and hairy tickled the top of Mom's head.

Yuck giggled. The spider was hanging on a thread from the ceiling, crawling in Mom's hair.

"Uurrgghh!" Mom shouted.

"Quick, get it!" Polly screamed.

"It's only trying to be friendly," Yuck told them.

The spider dropped onto the floor.

"Squash it," Polly screamed, stamping her foot.

But the spider was much too quick for her. One second it was there, and the next it had gone.

"You scared it, Polly," Yuck told her.

"I hate spiders," Polly said, and she ran out of the kitchen.

Yuck got down on his hands and knees and started searching for the spider.

He couldn't find it anywhere.

"Hurry up or you'll be late for school," Mom said, handing him his bag.

When Yuck arrived at class, he raced to his seat next to Little Eric. "I saw a spider," he whispered.

Mrs. Wagon the Dragon was standing at the front of the classroom.

"No talking, Yuck!" she said. "This week is Reading Week! I want you all to follow me to the library!"

Everyone stood up and followed the Dragon out into the corridor.

"It was a big, fat, hairy, scary spider," Yuck whispered.

"Did you touch it?" Little Eric asked.

The Dragon opened the library door.

"I want each of you to choose a book," she said. "Then find a seat and read quietly."

The school library was full of row upon row of books on every subject.

"Can we choose any

book we want, Mrs. Wagon?" Schoolie Julie asked.

"As long as it's not a picture book," the Dragon said. "And make sure you read it from cover to cover."

Yuck and Little Eric looked along the bookshelves.

SHHH!! QUIET!

Each bookshelf was marked with a letter.

A: Aliens . . . Arithmetic . . . Art . . .

B: Balloons . . . Banjos . . . Basketball . . .

C: Cats . . . Computers . . . Cookery . . .

Yuck ran to the shelf marked *S*. He read along the titles and took down a little yellow book. "*Spiders*," he read, showing it to Little Eric.

They took the book to a table in the far corner and sat down to read it together. . . .

 # SPIDERS

Spiders have eight legs and
up to eight eyes. In the dark, they
use hairs on their bodies
to feel where they're going.

Spiders spin webs made of
silk thread that is twice as strong
as steel.

Spiders eat insects, and some
even chomp mice and birds.

Some spiders have a poisonous
bite, but only a few are harmful to
humans. For safety, ask
what type of spider it is
before touching it.

As they were reading, Little Eric noticed something crawling out of Yuck's bag.

"Look!" he said, pointing.

Yuck looked. It was the big, fat, hairy, scary spider!

"So THAT'S where it went!" Yuck said.

The spider crawled out of his bag and up the table leg.

"Is it poisonous?" Little Eric asked.

Yuck looked in his *Spiders* book. He pointed to a picture.

THE SCARY SPIDER
Scientific name: Spidercus scaricus
Description: Big, fat, and hairy

Yuck read what it said in the book. . . .

The Scary Spider is often mistaken
for the Poisonous Man-eating Spider,
Spidercus horribilus, because of its scary
appearance. However, this is a mistake. The
Scary Spider is nonpoisonous and very
friendly. It is only hairy because it likes to
be cuddled.

"It's friendly," Yuck said.

He gave the spider a stroke. "You're not really scary, are you? You're a nice spider."

The spider tickled Yuck's finger with its hairy leg.

Yuck decided that when he was EMPEROR OF EVERYTHING, he would appoint himself Lord Protector of Spiders. He'd live in a castle full of cobwebs and flies. Spiders would come from miles around to eat fly pie and sleep in hammocks made of silk. Anyone who was nasty to spiders would be squashed by THE GIANT FOOT.

At lunchtime, Yuck and Little Eric stood in the line for the cafeteria.

Frank the Tank and Clip-Clop Chloe were in front of them.

Yuck took the scary spider from his pocket and placed it on the counter by the knives and forks.

"A spider!" Frank the Tank screamed, running away.

"A scary spider!" Clip-Clop Chloe screamed, running after him.

"It's only trying to be friendly," Yuck called, picking the spider up.

Yuck and Little Eric took the last two burgers and sat down.

Yuck put the spider on his tray. While he ate his food, it scurried off to explore.

Polly Princess and Juicy Lucy were sitting at the table next to the teachers.

The spider scurried toward them.

"I've read two books today," Lucy said.

"I've read three," Polly told her.

The spider climbed the table leg.

"Miss Fortune says I'm probably the best reader in the whole school," Polly said. She gobbled her sausage and mashed potatoes.

"Aaaggghhh!" she screamed.

The big, fat, hairy, scary spider was crawling over her sausage.

Polly threw her fork down. "It's that SPIDER!" she shouted.

Mr. Reaper, the principal, stood up. "What's the matter, Polly?" he asked.

"It's Yuck, sir! It's his scary spider!"

Yuck ran over. "It's only trying to be friendly, sir."

"I hate spiders!" Polly said.

The spider scurried across the table.

The Reaper picked up an empty glass and turned it upside down. "Gotcha!" he said, trapping the spider with it.

He took a piece of paper from his pocket and slipped it under the glass. "Yuck, come to my office immediately!"

The Reaper picked up the glass with the spider in it, and carried it to his office.

"You must not bring spiders to school, Yuck," the Reaper said.

"But, Mr. Reaper! I didn't."

"Don't lie, Yuck."

"I didn't, sir. It crawled into my bag. It's not dangerous. It's a friendly spider."

The Reaper put the glass on the shelf  behind his desk. The scary spider was still trapped inside. It was trying to get out.

"Aren't you going to let it go, sir?" Yuck asked.

The Reaper grinned. "I hate spiders," he said.

He handed Yuck a pile of paper. "For your punishment, I want you to write out one HUNDRED times: *I must not bring spiders to school.*"

"But, Mr. Reaper—"

The Reaper booted Yuck out of his office.

That evening, Polly told Mom what had happened.

"Yuck took that spider to school!" she said. "Mr. Reaper's given him lines."

Mom sent Yuck to his room to do his punishment. But all Yuck could think about was the spider trapped under the glass.

He had to rescue it, but he needed some friends to help him.

Yuck opened the door to his wardrobe and looked inside. "We have an emergency," he said.

In the darkness, crawling among the cobwebs, was his Secret Army of Spiders, the S.A.S.

There were Micro Spiders and Gorilla Spiders, Crane Spiders, and Telescope Spiders. They were spinning parachutes, crawling up and down silk ropes, and jumping from coat hangers.

At the bottom of the wardrobe, spiders were marching eight legs at a time—left, left, left, left, right, right, right, right!

"General, are you there?" Yuck asked.

From the back of the closet, through a tangle of cobwebs, hobbled General Household Spider, the oldest spider in Yuck's collection.

He had one leg missing and carried a walking stick.

"I have a mission for the S.A.S.," Yuck said. "A rescue mission. It's going to take place tomorrow at lunchtime at school."

Yuck told General Household Spider his plan. . . .

The next morning, Yuck held tightly to his bag. The S.A.S. were hiding inside it.

When he arrived at school, the Reaper was waiting for him. He grabbed Yuck by the ear. "Have you done your lines, Yuck?"

"Er . . . a dog ate them, sir," Yuck said.

"What dog?"

"They blew away in a tornado, sir."

"Nonsense!"

"I was kidnapped by aliens, sir."

"Come with me, Yuck!"

The Reaper dragged Yuck to his office, and handed him another bundle of paper.

"For your punishment, I want you to write ONE THOUSAND times: *I must not bring spiders to school.*"

"One THOUSAND, sir?"

"You're to do them in the library at lunchtime!"

"But, Mr. Reaper, I can't. I'm busy this lunchtime."

"Tough," the Reaper said. "And I'll be checking up on you, so you'd better be there."

Yuck looked at the scary spider trapped under the glass on the Reaper's shelf.

It wasn't moving.

That lunchtime,

Yuck called a secret meeting in the playground. Fartin' Martin, Tom Butts, and Little
Eric gathered around. Yuck showed them the
huge bundle of paper that the Reaper had
given him.

"I have to stay in the library," he said.

Then he showed them the spiders in
his bag.

Fartin' Martin, Tom Butts, and Little Eric
all agreed to help.

"We'll have to work quickly," Yuck said.

Yuck raced off to the library while Little Eric ran to the art room and grabbed a pot of paint. Little Eric threw it out of the window to Tom Butts. Tom Butts rolled it across the playground to Fartin' Martin. Fartin' Martin passed the pot of paint through the library window to Yuck, who was waiting inside.

"Nice one," Yuck said. "Stay there until I give the signal."

Yuck grabbed the bundle of paper and spread the pages over the floor. He opened the pot of paint and unzipped his bag.

General Household Spider crawled out, followed by his troops.

"We have a minor delay," Yuck told them. He began writing: *I must not bring spiders to school.*

"Copy me," he said, pointing to the paint pot. The spiders scurried over and dipped their legs in the paint. They crawled out onto the paper scribbling, eight legs at a time. . . .

Just then, Yuck heard the door open.

It was Polly. She'd come to get a book. "What are YOU doing here?" she asked.

"My lines," Yuck said.

Polly looked at the sheets of paper on the floor. They were crawling with spiders.

"Aaarrrggghhh!" she screamed.

She turned and ran out of the library.

When she was gone, General Household Spider tapped Yuck's foot with his stick.

All Yuck's lines were written.

"Thank you," Yuck said.

He ran to the library window and General Household Spider followed with his troops.

Fartin' Martin and Tom Butts were waiting outside.

"Are you ready?" Yuck asked them.

"All clear," they replied.

"Good luck."

The S.A.S. crawled out, and Fartin' Martin and Tom Butts led the spiders along the side of the building to the Reaper's office. They peered through the window.

The Reaper was polishing a photograph of himself.

"Over there," Fartin' Martin whispered.

"Under the glass," Tom Butts said.

General Household Spider crawled up to the windowsill and looked in. The scary spider was on the shelf behind the Reaper.

Suddenly the office door burst open.

It was Polly.

Fartin' Martin and Tom Butts listened.

"Quick, Mr. Reaper, it's an emergency!" they heard. "Yuck's got spiders in the library!"

The Reaper ran out, slamming the door behind him.

"Over to you, General," Fartin' Martin whispered.

General Household Spider waved his troops in through a gap at the bottom of the window. The rescue mission began.

The Telescope Spiders went in first, lowering themselves down to the floor, looking out for danger with their eight eyes.

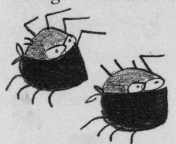

A ninja squad of black-backed Micro Spiders scattered up the walls and across the ceiling.

A commando squad of hairy-bottomed Gorilla Spiders swung in on silk threads, landing on the shelf where the scary spider was trapped.

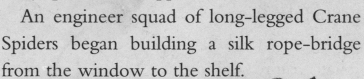

An engineer squad of long-legged Crane Spiders began building a silk rope-bridge from the window to the shelf.

Tom Butts looked at the clock on the Reaper's wall. The S.A.S. would have to complete the rescue before the headmaster returned.

Fartin' Martin ran back to the library window. "He's coming," he whispered to Yuck. "Good luck."

Yuck picked up the sheets of paper from the library floor and sat down at the table in the corner, pretending to write.

The Reaper opened the library door. "Where are they?" he demanded.

"Where are what, Mr. Reaper?" Yuck asked.

"The spiders," Polly said, running in behind the Reaper.

"I don't know what you're talking about," Yuck said.

He stood up and handed the Reaper the big stack of paper.

The Reaper stared at the pages. He saw the lines in tiny handwriting.

I must not bring spiders to school.
I must not bring spiders to school.
I must not bring spiders to school.
I must not bring spiders to school.
I must not bring spiders to school.

"There's a THOUSAND there," Yuck said. "You can count them if you want."

"That was fast," the Reaper said.

"I've been work-ing hard all lunch-time, sir. There are no spiders in here."

The Reaper scrunched up the bundle of paper and walked out of the library.

"He's lying, Mr. Reaper," Polly said, run-ning after the principal.

Meanwhile, Fartin' Martin and Tom Butts watched through the window as the S.A.S. set to work in the Reaper's office.

The Telescope Spiders kept a lookout under the door as General Household Spider directed each squad into position.

The Micro Spiders lowered silk threads from the ceiling. The Gorilla Spiders attached the threads to the glass. The Crane Spiders secured the silk rope-bridge.

General Household Spider pointed his stick and gave the signal to begin.

The Micro Spiders pulled their threads and lifted the glass. The Gorilla Spiders dashed underneath the glass and dragged the scary spider out. It was weak and could hardly move. The Crane Spiders rushed across the bridge carrying a silk stretcher.

Just then, the Telescope Spiders signaled from the door that someone was coming. General Household Spider pointed his stick to the window and the S.A.S. moved out.

The Micro Spiders let down their threads and lowered the glass back into place. The Gorilla Spiders lifted the scary spider onto the stretcher and the Crane Spiders carried it across the rope-bridge. They all pulled the bridge up and left through the window.

Fartin' Martin and Tom Butts cheered.

The S.A.S. had done it! The scary spider was saved!

Yuck was leaning out of the library window.

"Mission accomplished," Fartin' Martin called to him. He ran over and handed Yuck the scary spider. "See you in a minute," he said.

The scary spider was beginning to move again. Yuck carefully placed it in his pocket, and the S.A.S. crawled back into his bag. Yuck smiled and ran out of the library door.

Little Eric was waiting for him in the corridor. "Let's go," he said.

Everyone was heading to class.

Yuck and Little Eric ran down the corridor and watched as the Reaper opened the door to his office.

Polly was with him. "Yuck has got spiders, Mr. Reaper. I saw them," she said.

"It's gone!" the Reaper shouted.

"What's gone, sir?" Polly asked.

"The scary spider!"

Yuck and Little Eric were giggling in the corridor.

"Yuck!" the Reaper called.

"Yes, sir? Is something the matter?"

"Did you take that scary spider from my office?"

"Me, Mr. Reaper? I've been in the library all lunchtime, sir."

Fartin' Martin and Tom Butts came running down the corridor.

"Maybe it escaped, Mr. Reaper," Fartin' Martin said, giggling.

"Escaped?"

"A scary spider's on the loose!" Tom Butts said.

"A scary, poison- ous spider!" Little Eric said.

"A scary, poison- ous, man-eating spider!" Yuck said.

Everyone in the corridor began running.

"There's a scary spider on the loose!" they screamed.

"No, there isn't. It's Yuck fooling around!" Polly shouted.

"Everyone go to your classrooms!" the Reaper told them. "If you see a spider, tell me at once!"

The Reaper picked up the glass and went on the hunt.

"Just you wait, Yuck," Polly said. "You're going to be in BIG TROUBLE."

Yuck giggled as he went into class.

"It's Polly who's going to be in BIG TROUBLE," he said to his friends.

That night, Yuck opened his bag and let all the spiders run around in his room.

The scary spider was weak. It climbed up onto Yuck's bed and he stroked it better.

"There, there," he said. "How could Polly and the Reaper be so nasty? You're not really scary."

The scary spider tickled Yuck's finger.

"Tomorrow we're going to teach the Reaper a lesson. And Polly, too. We're going to set a trap," he said.

"General," he called.

General Household Spider hobbled over on his stick, and Yuck whispered his plan.

The General gathered his troops.

That night, while Mom, Dad, and Polly were asleep, the S.A.S. began spinning, yard after yard of triple-thick, superstrong silk thread.

They built a huge web the size of Yuck's carpet.

Carefully, Yuck rolled it up and packed it in his school bag.

General Household Spider gave the signal and the S.A.S. scurried out of Yuck's door.

Yuck followed them to Polly's room.

Polly was asleep.

The spiders scurried across her bedroom floor, up the leg of her bed, and over her duvet.

General Household Spider went first. He hobbled over Polly's ear and crawled across her face. He stood on her nose, peering into her mouth.

Polly's mouth was open. She was snoring.

"Good luck, General," Yuck whispered. "See you tomorrow."

General Household Spider waved his stick.
He jumped into Polly's mouth.

One by one, the S.A.S. followed. Spider
after spider crawled over Polly's face and
jumped into her mouth.

Last of all, the big, fat, hairy, scary spider
crawled onto Polly's chin. It waved to Yuck,
then squeezed in with
everyone else. With
one leg poking up,
it tickled Polly's lips.

Polly's mouth closed.

Yuck giggled and crept
out.

In the morning, when Yuck woke up,

Polly was standing in the doorway to his room. She was hiccuping.

"Where are they . . . HIC?" she asked.

"Where are what?" Yuck giggled.

"Your spiders!"

"I don't know what you're talking about, Polly," Yuck said.

Polly picked up the *Spiders* book by his 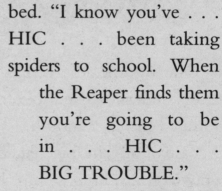 bed. "I know you've . . . HIC . . . been taking spiders to school. When the Reaper finds them you're going to be in . . . HIC . . . BIG TROUBLE."

Polly stormed out and Yuck giggled.

"Get up, Yuck!" Mom called.

Yuck got dressed and left for school with Polly.

When they arrived, Polly went straight to the library to choose an extra book before class.

Yuck ran to the playground.

Fartin' Martin, Tom Butts, and Little Eric were waiting for him. He gave them the rolled-up spiderweb from his bag.

"Quick, Polly's getting a book," he said.

Fartin' Martin, Tom Butts, and Little Eric raced off to the library.

Meanwhile, Yuck went to find the Reaper. He was at the edge of the playground, searching in the bushes. "Have you found that scary spider, Mr. Reaper?" Yuck asked.

"Not yet, but I will," the Reaper told him. He was clutching the empty glass.

"I'll help you," Yuck said.

Outside the library, Little Eric waited in the corridor, checking that no one was coming.

Quietly, Fartin' Martin opened the library door.

Tom Butts unrolled the giant spiderweb.

He stood on Fartin' Martin's shoulders and pinned it up. Fartin' Martin held him steady as he stretched it across the doorway.

Inside, Polly was choosing a book from the shelf marked *P*.

Fartin' Martin gave the signal that everything was ready, and Little Eric raced outside.

He ran across the playground to the Reaper. "Quick, Mr. Reaper!" he said. "Polly's got spiders in the library!"

"Polly?" the Reaper asked.

Behind the Reaper's back, Yuck gave the thumbs-up.

"Yes, sir—lots of them," Little Eric said. "Quick, Mr. Reaper, run!"

The Reaper ran as fast as he could across the playground and down the corridor to the library.

"Is the trap set?" Yuck asked Little Eric.

"Everything's ready," Little Eric said.

They ran to watch.

"Mr. Reaper! What's happened?" Polly asked, turning round.

The Reaper was stuck in the web!

"Get me out of here!" he shouted.

The Reaper wriggled and struggled.

"Are you all right, sir?" Polly asked.

"It's your spiders!" the Reaper said.

"But I haven't got any spiders. I hate spi—
HIC."

Polly hiccupped and General Household
Spider crawled out of her mouth.

"Aaagghh!" she screamed.

General Household Spider hobbled up to
the web, and crawled onto the Reaper.

"Get it off me!" the Reaper cried.

He was trapped.

Yuck, Fartin' Martin, Tom Butts, and Little Eric were standing in the corridor, giggling.

"What's happening?" Yuck asked.

". . . HIC." A Gorilla Spider swung out of Polly's mouth on a silk thread and landed on the Reaper.

". . . HIC . . . HIC . . . HIC!" A long line of spiders marched out of Polly's mouth— left, left, left, left, right, right, right, right!

"AAAGGGHHH!" the Reaper shouted, as they scurried onto the web, crawling up and down his arms and legs, inside his shirt and over his face. They ran up his pants and into his ears.

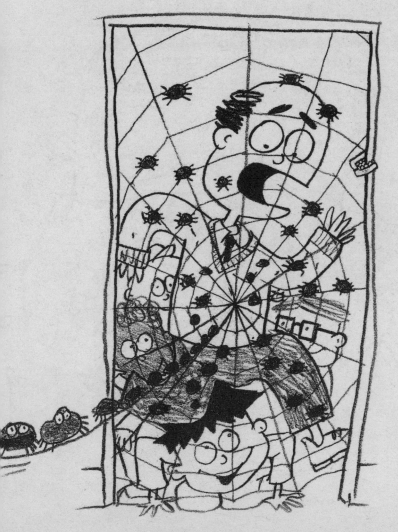

"Get them off me!" the Reaper begged. "I hate spiders!"

Polly burped and the big, fat, hairy, scary spider popped out of her mouth.

Yuck peered through the web.

"There it is, Mr. Reaper," he said, laughing. "It's not me who's been bringing spiders to school. It's Polly!"

CHECK OUT YUCK'S NEXT ADVENTURE!

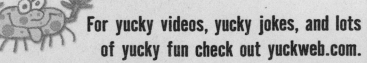